Russell Hoban

# How Tom
# Beat Captain Najork
## and his
# Hired Sportsmen

Illustrated by
Quentin Blake

Jonathan Cape
Thirty Bedford Square London

*also by Russell Hoban and Quentin Blake*
A NEAR THING FOR CAPTAIN NAJORK
ACE DRAGON LTD
THE TWENTY ELEPHANT RESTAURANT

*also by Russell Hoban*
HARVEY'S HIDEOUT
THE MOLE FAMILY'S CHRISTMAS

*also by Quentin Blake*
PATRICK
JACK AND NANCY
ANGELO
SNUFF
MR MAGNOLIA

First published 1974
Reprinted 1983
Text © 1974 by Yankee Rover Inc.
Illustrations © 1974 by Quentin Blake

Jonathan Cape Ltd,
30 Bedford Square, London WC1

ISBN 0 224 00999 0

Printed in Italy by New Interlitho, SpA, Milan

Tom lived with his maiden aunt, Miss Fidget Wonkham-Strong.
She wore an iron hat, and took no nonsense from anyone.
Where she walked the flowers drooped, and when she sang the
trees all shivered.

Tom liked to fool around. He fooled around with sticks and
stones and crumpled paper, with mewses and passages and
dustbins, with bent nails and broken glass and holes in fences.

He fooled around with mud, and stomped and squelched and slithered through it.

He fooled around on high-up things that shook and wobbled and teetered.

He fooled around with dropping things from bridges into rivers and fishing them out.

He fooled around with barrels in alleys

When Aunt Fidget Wonkham-Strong asked him what
he was doing, Tom said that he was fooling around.

"It looks very like playing to me," said Aunt Fidget
Wonkham-Strong. "Too much playing is not good, and you play
too much. You had better stop it and do something useful."

"All right," said Tom.

But he did not stop. He did a little
fooling around with two or three
cigar bands and a paper-clip.

At dinner Aunt Fidget Wonkham-
Strong, wearing her iron hat, said,
"Eat your mutton and your
cabbage-and-potato sog."
"All right," said Tom. He ate it.

After dinner Aunt Fidget
Wonkham-Strong said, "Now learn
off pages 65 to 75 of the Nautical
Almanac, and that will teach
you not to fool around so much."
"All right," said Tom.
He learned them off.

"From now on I shall keep an eye on you," Aunt Fidget Wonkham-Strong said, "and if you do not stop fooling around I shall send for Captain Najork and his hired sportsmen."

"Who is Captain Najork?" said Tom.

"Captain Najork," said Aunt Fidget Wonkham-Strong, "is seven feet tall, with eyes like fire, a voice like thunder, and a handlebar moustache. His trousers are always freshly pressed, his blazer is immaculate, his shoes are polished mirror-bright, and he is every inch a terror. When Captain Najork is sent for he comes up the river in his pedal boat, with his hired sportsmen all pedalling hard. He teaches fooling-around boys the lesson they so badly need, and it is not one that they soon forget."

Aunt Fidget Wonkham-Strong kept an eye on Tom. He did not stop fooling around. He did low and muddy fooling around and he did high and wobbly fooling around. He fooled around with dropping things off bridges and he fooled around with barrels in alleys.

"Very well," said Aunt Fidget Wonkham-Strong at table in her iron hat. "Eat your greasy bloaters."

Tom ate them.

"I have warned you," said Aunt Fidget Wonkham-Strong, "that I should send for Captain Najork if you did not stop fooling around. I have done that. As you like to play so much, you shall play against Captain Najork and his hired sportsmen. They play hard games and they play them jolly hard. Prepare yourself."

"All right," said Tom. He fooled around with a bottle-top
and a burnt match.

The next day Captain Najork came up the river with his hired
sportsmen pedalling his pedal boat.

They came ashore smartly, carrying an immense brown-paper parcel. They marched into the garden, one, two, three, four. Captain Najork was only six feet tall. His eyes were not like fire, his voice was not like thunder.

"Right," said Captain Najork. "Where is the sportive infant?"

"There," said Aunt Fidget Wonkham-Strong.

"Here," said Tom.

"Right," said the Captain. "We shall play womble, muck, and sneedball, in that order." The hired sportsmen sniggered as they undid the immense brown-paper parcel, set up the womble run, the ladders and the net, and distributed the rakes and stakes.

"How do you play womble?" said Tom.

"You'll find out," said Captain Najork.

"Who's on my side?" said Tom.

"Nobody," said Captain Najork. "Let's get started."

Womble turned out to be a shaky, high-up, wobbling and teetering sort of a game, and Tom was used to that kind of fooling around. The Captain's side raked first. Tom staked. The hired sportsmen played so hard that they wombled too fast, and were shaky with the rakes. Tom fooled around the way he always did, and all his stakes dropped true. When it was his turn to rake he did not let Captain Najork and the hired sportsmen score a single rung, and at the end of the snetch he won by six ladders.

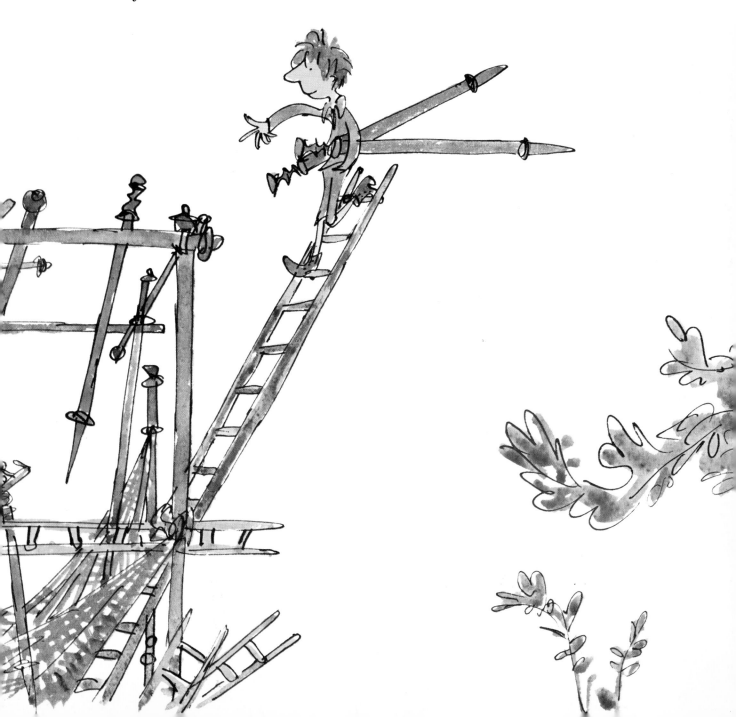

"Right," said Captain Najork, clenching his teeth. "Muck next. Same sides."

The court was laid out at.low tide in the river mud. Tom mucked first, and slithered through the marks while the hired sportsmen poled and shovelled. Tom had fooled around with mud so much that he scored time after time.

Captain Najork's men poled too hard and shovelled too fast and
tired themselves out. Tom just mucked about and fooled around,
and when the tide came in he led the opposition 673 to 49.

"Really," said Aunt Fidget Wonkham-Strong to Captain
Najork, "you must make an effort to teach this boy a lesson."

"Some boys learn hard," said the Captain, chewing his
moustache. "Now for sneedball."

The hired sportsmen brought out the ramp, the slide, the barrel, the bobble, the sneeding tongs, the bar, and the grapples. Tom saw at once that sneedball was like several kinds of fooling around that he was particularly good at. Partly it was like dropping things off bridges into rivers and fishing them out and partly it was like fooling around with barrels in alleys.

"I had better tell you," said the Captain to Tom, "that I played in the Sneedball Finals five years running."

"They couldn't have been very final if you had to keep doing it for five years," said Tom. He motioned the Captain aside, away from Aunt Fidget Wonkham-Strong. "Let's make this interesting," he said.

"What do you mean?" said the Captain.

"Let's play *for* something," said Tom. "Let's say if I win I get your pedal boat."

"What do I get if *I* win?" said the Captain. "Because I am certainly going to win *this* one."

"You can have Aunt Fidget Wonkham-Strong," said Tom.

"She's impressive," said the Captain. "I admit that freely. A very impressive lady."

"She fancies you," said Tom. "I can tell by the way she looks sideways at you from underneath her iron hat."

"No!" said the Captain.

"Yes," said Tom.

"And you'll part with her if she'll have me?" said the Captain.

"It's the only sporting thing to do," said Tom.

"Agreed then!" said the Captain. "By George! I'm almost sorry that I'm going to have to teach you a lesson by beating you at sneedball."

"Let's get started," said Tom.

The hired sportsmen had first slide. Captain Najork himself barrelled, and he and his men played like demons. But Tom tonged the bobble in the same fooling-around way that he fished things out of rivers, and he quickly moved into the lead. Captain Najork sweated big drops, and he slid his barrel too hard so it hit the stop and slopped over. But Tom just fooled around, and when it was his slide he never spilled a drop.

Darkness fell, but they shot up flares and went on playing. By three o'clock in the morning Tom had won by 85 to 10. As the last flare went up above the garden he looked down from the ramp at the defeated Captain and his hired sportsmen and he said, "Maybe that will teach you not to fool around with a boy who knows how to fool around."

Captain Najork broke down and wept, but Aunt Fidget Wonkham-Strong had him put to bed and brought him peppermint tea, and then he felt better.

Tom took his boat and pedalled
to the next town down the
river. There he advertised
in the newspaper for a new aunt.
When he found one that he liked,
he told her, "No greasy
bloaters, no mutton and no
cabbage-and-potato sog. No
Nautical Almanac. And I do lots
of fooling around. Those are
my conditions."

The new aunt's name was Bundlejoy Cosysweet. She had a floppy hat with flowers on it. She had long, long hair.

"That sounds fine to me," she said. "We'll have a go."

Aunt Fidget Wonkham-Strong married Captain Najork even though he had lost the sneedball game, and they were very happy together. She made the hired sportsmen learn off pages of the Nautical Almanac every night after dinner.